Jo

Speedboat

Speedboat

James Marshall

1 9 7 6

Houghton Mifflin Company, Boston

Library of Congress Cataloging in Publication Data

Marshall, James, 1942-
    Speedboat.

    SUMMARY: Jasper Raisintoast, friend of Tweedy-Jones,
zooms into trouble and adventure in his superfast, shiny
speedboat.
    [1. Boats and boating--Fiction. 2. Friendship--Fic-
tion] I. Title.
PZ7.M35672Sp   [Fic]   75-40349
ISBN 0-395-24384-X

For Scrooge

CHAPTER ONE

Jasper Raisintoast was up bright
and early.

He was full of pep.

"What a swell day to speed
up the river in my speedboat,"
he said to his pal Jack Tweedy-Jones.

"Want to come along?"

"Certainly not," said Tweedy-Jones.

"None of that racing around for me!"

Tweedy-Jones did not like speedboats.

"Loud, horrid machines," he said.

He much preferred relaxing

in his favorite armchair.

Tweedy-Jones was a homebody.

Outside, Raisintoast was revving up
his speedboat.

"I'll be home in time for supper,"
he called to Tweedy-Jones.

"See that you are," his pal answered
through the window. "And try
to stay out of trouble!"

Poor Tweedy-Jones was always
worrying about Raisintoast.

"He's forever getting himself
into mischief."

Really, it was a wonder that
they had been friends for so long.

"But maybe friends don't *have*
to like the same things," he thought.

In a flash, the Raisintoast craft

was on its way.

It made lots of noise.

Tweedy-Jones stood at the window

and watched the boat disappear

around the bend.

"Loud, horrid machines," he muttered.

CHAPTER TWO

"Here comes that Raisintoast,"
grumbled people on the bank.
"Raisintoast is the biggest menace
on the river."
"He spoils the swimming."
"And listen to that racket!"
"Down with Raisintoast!"

They shook their fists in the air:

"Down with Raisintoast!!"

Raisintoast's speedboat caused such

a racket that he couldn't hear.

But he did see hands in the air.

He waved to everyone.

"Nice, friendly people," he said.

THE RIVER FOX

CHAPTER THREE

Around lunchtime Raisintoast's
stomach began to rumble.
"Gee whillikers, I'm really hungry,"
he thought.
Just around the bend he noticed
a little person stirring a big pot.
The pot was steaming.

Raisintoast's mouth began to water.

"Ummm, ummm, ummm, I'll bet

that's a hearty fish stew he's got

in that pot," he thought.

The boat drew up to the bank.

"Hi!" called out Raisintoast.

The little person kept on stirring.

"Ummm, ummm," thought Raisintoast,
"This will be a lovely change from
Tweedy-Jones' cooking. I was getting
tired of mutton and roast potatoes."
His mouth was watering even more.
"May I have a taste of that, please?" he
begged the little person.
The little person handed him the
big ladle.
Raisintoast closed his eyes and
took a great big gulp.
"I love stew," thought Raisintoast.
The little person watched silently.
Suddenly — Patoooee! Raisintoast
spat it all out.

"The worst stew I've *ever* tasted!"

He felt all queasy inside and ran

to his speedboat.

The little person watched him leave.

"Why should anyone want to taste

my soapy laundry water?" he

thought, scratching his head.

CHAPTER FOUR

Farther up the river Raisintoast
noticed an arts and crafts show.
"I'll buy a gift for Tweedy-Jones,"
thought Raisintoast. "He is so
fond of surprises."
Raisintoast docked his speedboat
and stepped onto the bank.

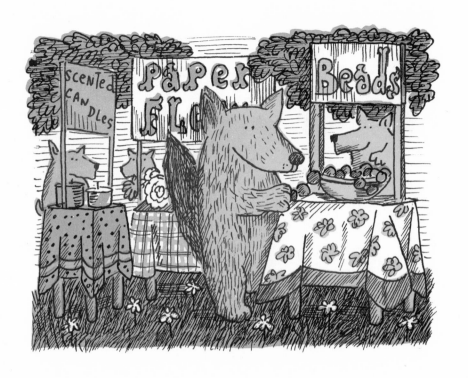

So many pretty things to look at!
Raisintoast examined Indian
moccasins, patchwork quilts, beads,
paper flowers, hand-painted
neckties, and wooden whistles.
But he was not satisfied.
"Nothing is right for Tweedy-Jones."

Then he came to the last booth.

A painter was painting pictures.

He was very, very good, and

Raisintoast was impressed.

"I have an idea," he thought.

"Can you paint my picture?"

he asked the painter.

"Don't be silly," said the painter.

"Of course I can, but only if you

take me for a spin in your boat."

"Agreed," said Raisintoast.

He sat down to have his picture

painted.

"Now sit perfectly still,"

said the painter.

Sitting still was very difficult.

Raisintoast was very excited.

"What a present for Tweedy-Jones!"

Later Raisintoast kept his promise.

He took the painter for a spin.

"That scared the pants off of me,"

said the painter.

CHAPTER FIVE

Later in the day Raisintoast came

to a bridge.

On the bridge stood a lady.

She had a small mustache.

She looked mean.

"Not so fast, you little runt!"

she called to Raisintoast.

Raisintoast stopped his engine.

"Where do you think you're going?"
bellowed the lady.

"Under the bridge and up the river,"
answered Raisintoast.

"Oh no you don't!" said she. "Not
without giving me a kiss first!"
Raisintoast shuddered.

He didn't like kissing mean ladies.

"I'd rather not," he said. "Thanks
just the same."

"I'll bop you on the head,"
said the lady.

"I'd rather not," he said.

"I'm waiting," said the lady.

"I'm doomed," thought Raisintoast.

"What would Tweedy-Jones do in a situation like this?"

The boat came near the bridge.

The lady bent over the railing; she shut her eyes and puckered her lips.

"I know!" thought Raisintoast.

He kissed the lady's chubby hand.

"What was that?" asked the lady,

opening her eyes.

"That's the way they kiss in Spain,

sometimes," said Raisintoast.

"Well I don't like it," said the lady.

"It tickles!"

And she bopped poor Raisintoast.

"Give me a *real* kiss, or I won't

let you pass."

Raisintoast decided to turn back.

The lady watched him leave.

"You little brat," she called out.

"I'll catch you *next* time!"

CHAPTER SIX

At home a cozy fire was crackling
and popping in the fireplace.
Tweedy-Jones was relaxing and
reading a new book called
How to Fly a Dirigible.
"That's not for me," he yawned.
And in a moment, he was asleep.

After his snooze Tweedy-Jones went
to his garden to water his favorite
flowers, his Johnny-jump-ups.
He heard a rap at the garden gate.
"Hi, Mr. Tweedy-Jones. Want to buy
some bubble gum?" said a child.
"Sweet child," thought Tweedy-Jones.

Now everyone loves bubble gum.

But when Tweedy-Jones blew a large

bubble, he felt something unusual.

His feet were no longer touching

the garden path.

And up he went!

Up and over the garden wall.

Up and over the tree tops.

"My stars," said Tweedy-Jones.

"What a curious feeling."

Some greenbirds flew up to see

what was going on.

"Isn't flying fun?" they asked

Tweedy-Jones, who didn't answer.

Far below things were getting
smaller and smaller.

"Raisintoast won't believe this,"
thought Tweedy-Jones.

A dirigible passed gracefully by.
People at the windows waved to
Tweedy-Jones, who waved back.

Suddenly Tweedy-Jones heard a loud

Pop!

A greenbird had popped his bubble!

And down he went!

Far below things were getting

larger and larger.

"I'm doomed!" thought Tweedy-Jones.

"What would Raisintoast do in a situation like this?"

People watched from the dirigible.

"He's a goner," they said.

"I've got it!" thought Tweedy-Jones.

Quickly he chewed his bubble gum.

He blew a second huge bubble.

Just in the nick of time!

Tweedy-Jones stopped falling so fast.

Gracefully he glided to earth,

landing in his very own garden.

"My stars!" exclaimed Tweedy-Jones.

"What an exhausting adventure!"

And he went inside for another nap.

CHAPTER SEVEN

Raisintoast was speeding homeward.

Rounding a bend in the river

he saw the loveliest creature.

She was sunning herself.

"I think I'll impress her," thought

Raisintoast.

Raisintoast was quite the show-off.

"I'll do my very best tricks."

The lovely creature heard the loud
noise and looked his way.

Raisintoast revved up his engine
and went round and round.

He smiled at the lovely creature,
who didn't smile back.

"I'll try something more difficult,"
thought Raisintoast. "I'll show her
what big waves I can make."

The speedboat dashed up the river
and back again, causing big waves
to splash on the bank.

The lovely creature got all wet.

She *still* wasn't smiling.

Raisintoast did a little dance
on the prow of the speedboat.
He stood on his head.
Finally the lovely creature waved
for Raisintoast to join her.
"My name is Jasper Raisintoast,"
he said, taking a deep bow.

The lovely creature smiled.

"And my name is Sheriff Mackenzie."

Raisintoast shook all over, while

Sheriff Mackenzie wrote out tickets

for river-speeding, foolishness, and

disturbing the peace of the river.

"I'm sorry," said Raisintoast.

CHAPTER EIGHT

Raisintoast and Tweedy-Jones were
happy to see each other.

"What a thoughtful present,"
said Tweedy-Jones when he saw the
nifty painting of his pal. "It looks
just like you."

He hung it over the fireplace.

As a special treat, Tweedy-Jones
served a tasty meal of mutton
and roast potatoes, while Raisintoast
talked about his adventures.
Tweedy-Jones knew that Raisintoast
would never believe *his* adventure.
"My day had its ups and downs,"
he said.

After dinner the pals went to bed.

"Tomorrow," yawned Raisintoast,

"I will go sky-diving."

"Be sure to take some bubble gum,"

said Tweedy-Jones.

But Raisintoast was sound asleep.

Tweedy-Jones turned off the light.